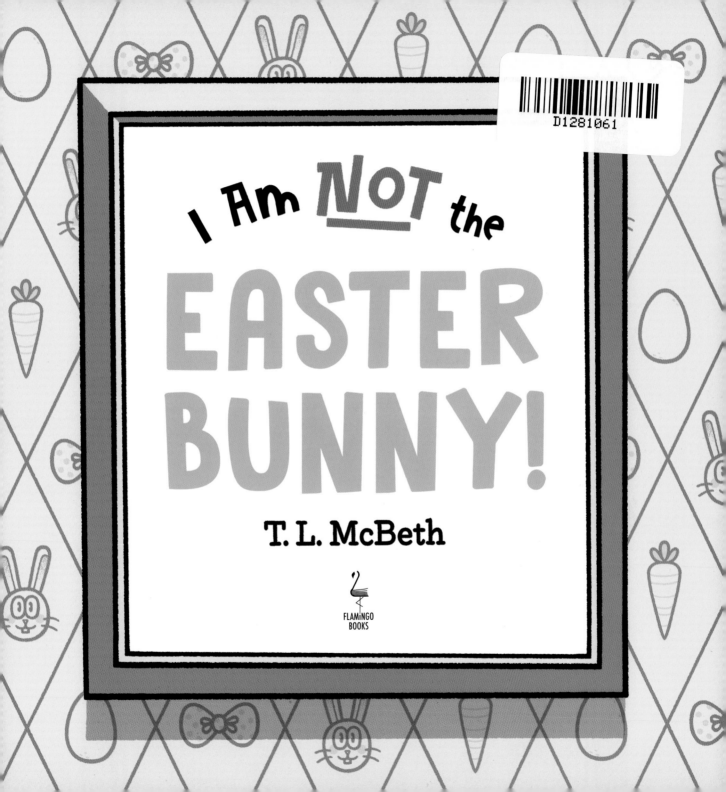

I Am NOT the EASTER BUNNY!

T. L. McBeth

FLAMINGO BOOKS

Everyone, look!
It's the Easter Bunny.

You must be the Easter Bunny.
You look just like him!

But look, you have a perfectly white coat and a fluffy cotton tail— just like the Easter Bunny!

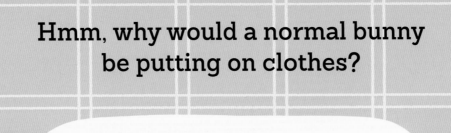

I've never seen a normal bunny wear a vest.

Lots of bunnies wear vests!
They are very cool and fashionable and
great for mild spring weather!

Name one other bunny
who wears a vest.

My friend Leonard wears a vest!

Who's Leonard?

See, you are the Easter Bunny—
you have an Easter basket!

Aha! If you're not the Easter Bunny, then why are you buying Easter eggs?!

That's an awfully suspicious grocery list . . .

But if you aren't the Easter Bunny—

All right, I've had just about enough of this! You've been bothering me all day—you followed me to the grocery store, into my house, and now you've ruined my arts and crafts project! For the last time, I am NOT the Easter Bunny!

Okay, okay. It's just that it would be SO EXCITING
to meet the actual Easter Bunny, you know?
But I guess you're just a regular bunny.
I'll leave you alone.

FLAMINGO BOOKS
An imprint of Penguin Random House LLC, New York

First published in the United States of America by Flamingo Books,
an imprint of Penguin Random House LLC, 2024

Visit us online at PenguinRandomHouse.com.

Library of Congress Cataloging-in-Publication Data is available.

ISBN 9780593528457

10 9 8 7 6 5 4 3 2 1

Manufactured in China

HH

Design by Lily K. Qian
Text set in Sanchez Slab

This book was made digitally using Procreate and Photoshop.